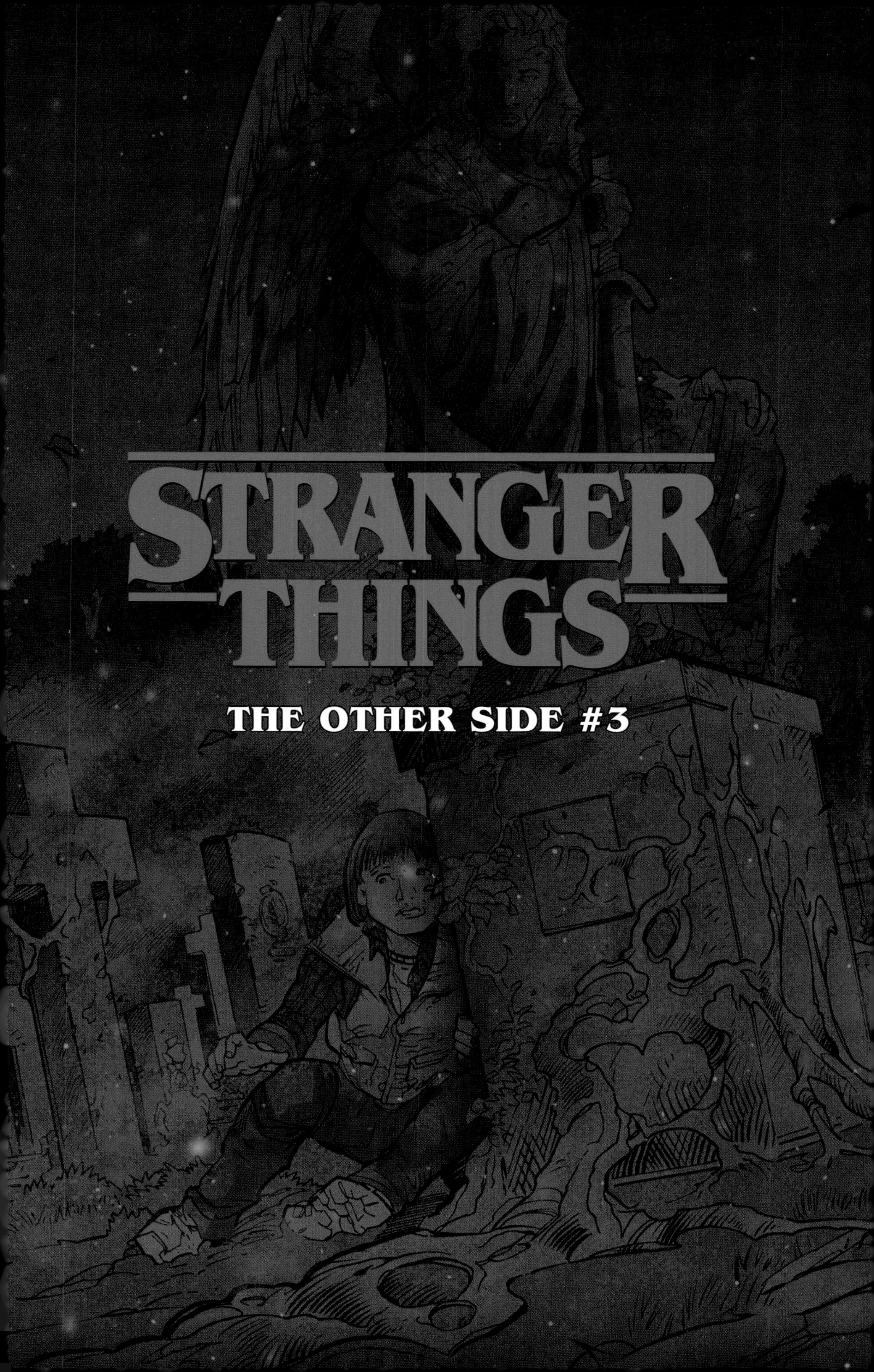
STRANGER THINGS
THE OTHER SIDE #3

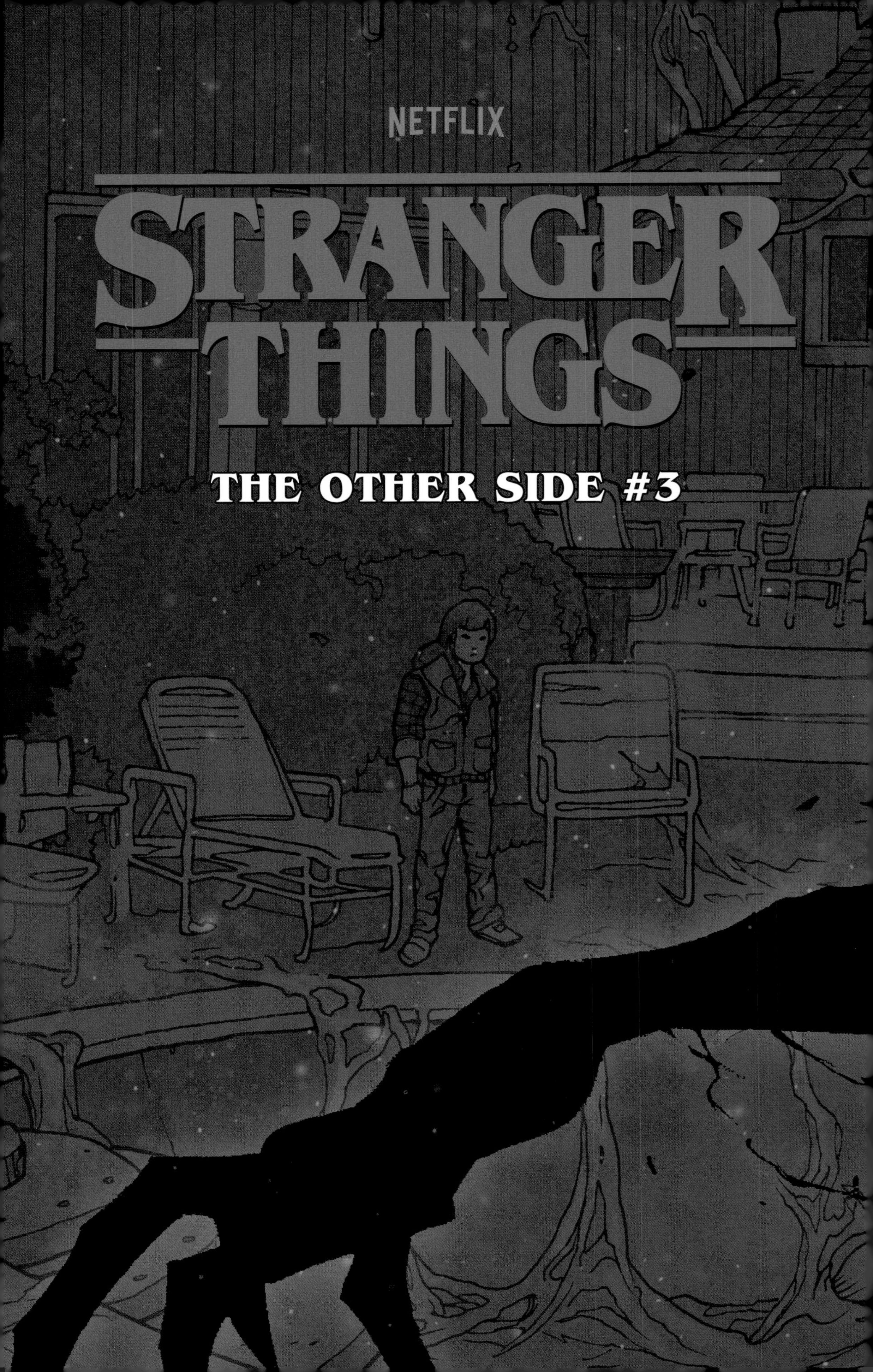
NETFLIX
STRANGER THINGS
THE OTHER SIDE #3

script
JODY HOUSER

pencils
STEFANO MARTINO

inks
KEITH CHAMPAGNE

colors
LAUREN AFFE

lettering
NATE PIEKOS OF BLAMBOT®

front cover art by
ALEKSI BRICLOT

ABDO Spotlight

DARK HORSE BOOKS

ABDOBOOKS.COM

Reinforced library bound edition published in 2020 by Spotlight, a division of ABDO, PO Box 398166, Minneapolis, Minnesota 55439. Spotlight produces high-quality reinforced library bound editions for schools and libraries.
Published by agreement with Dark Horse Comics.

Printed in the United States of America, North Mankato, Minnesota.
042019
092019

 THIS BOOK CONTAINS RECYCLED MATERIALS

Library of Congress Control Number: 2019939089

Publisher's Cataloging-in-Publication Data

Names: Houser, Jody, author. | Martino, Stefano; Champagne, Keith; Affe, Lauren, illustrators.
Title: The other side / writer: Jody Houser; art: Stefano Martino; Keith Champagne; Lauren Affe.
Description: Minneapolis, Minnesota: Spotlight, 2020 | Series: Stranger things
Summary: This spine-tingling comic based on the hit Netflix series follows Will Byers' struggle to survive in the treacherous Upside Down.
Identifiers: ISBN 9781532143878 (#1; lib. bdg.) | ISBN 9781532143885 (#2; lib. bdg.) | ISBN 9781532143892 (#3; lib. bdg.) | ISBN 9781532143908 (#4; lib. bdg.)
Subjects: LCSH: Stranger things (Television program)--Juvenile fiction. | Science fiction television programs--Juvenile fiction. | Supernatural disappearances--Juvenile fiction. | Monsters--Juvenile fiction. | Graphic novels--Juvenile fiction. | Comic books, strips, etc.--Juvenile fiction
Classification: DDC 741.5--dc2

Spotlight

A Division of ABDO
abdobooks.com

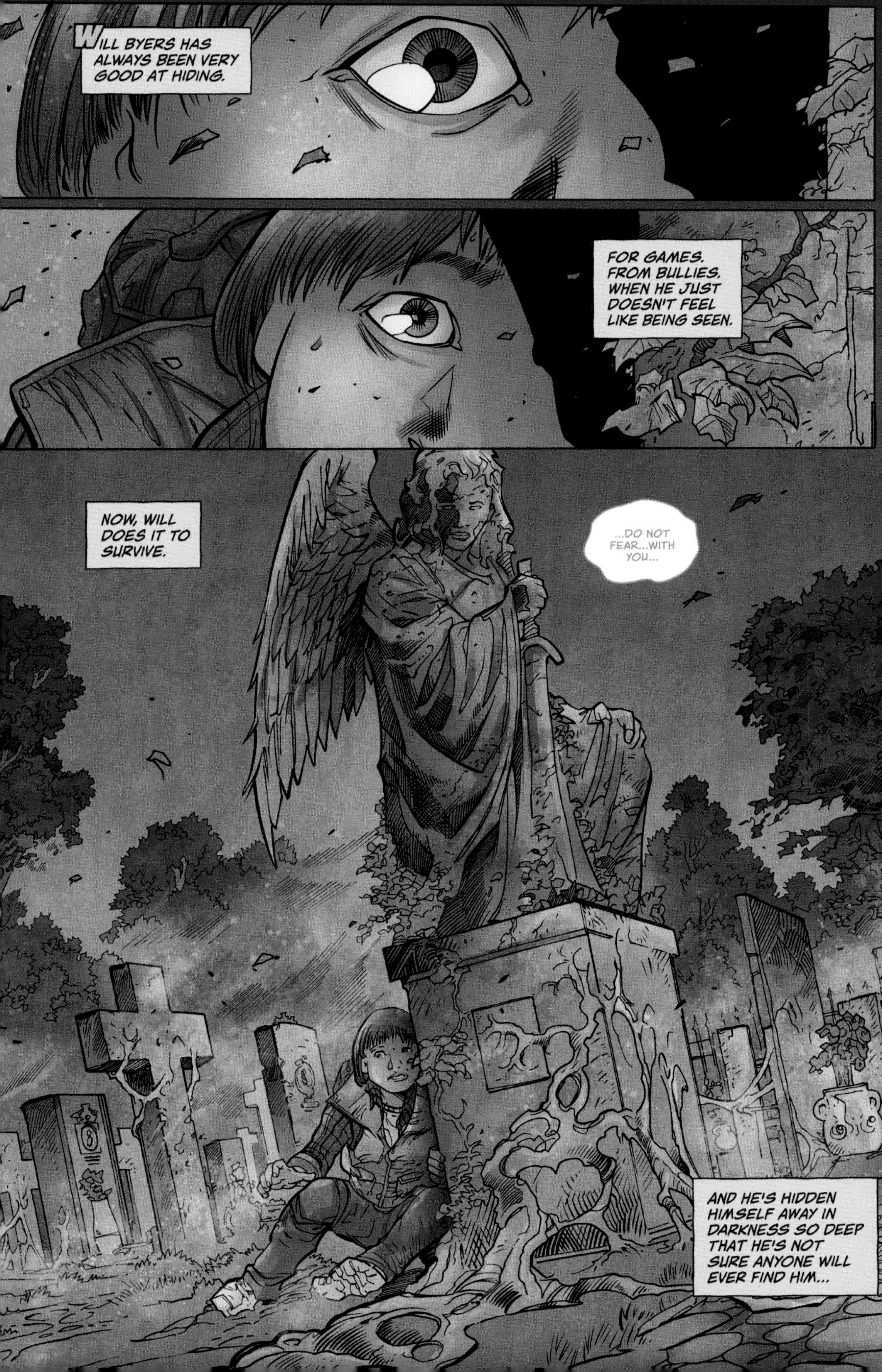
WILL BYERS HAS ALWAYS BEEN VERY GOOD AT HIDING.
FOR GAMES. FROM BULLIES. WHEN HE JUST DOESN'T FEEL LIKE BEING SEEN.
NOW, WILL DOES IT TO SURVIVE.
...DO NOT FEAR...WITH YOU...
AND HE'S HIDDEN HIMSELF AWAY IN DARKNESS SO DEEP THAT HE'S NOT SURE ANYONE WILL EVER FIND HIM...

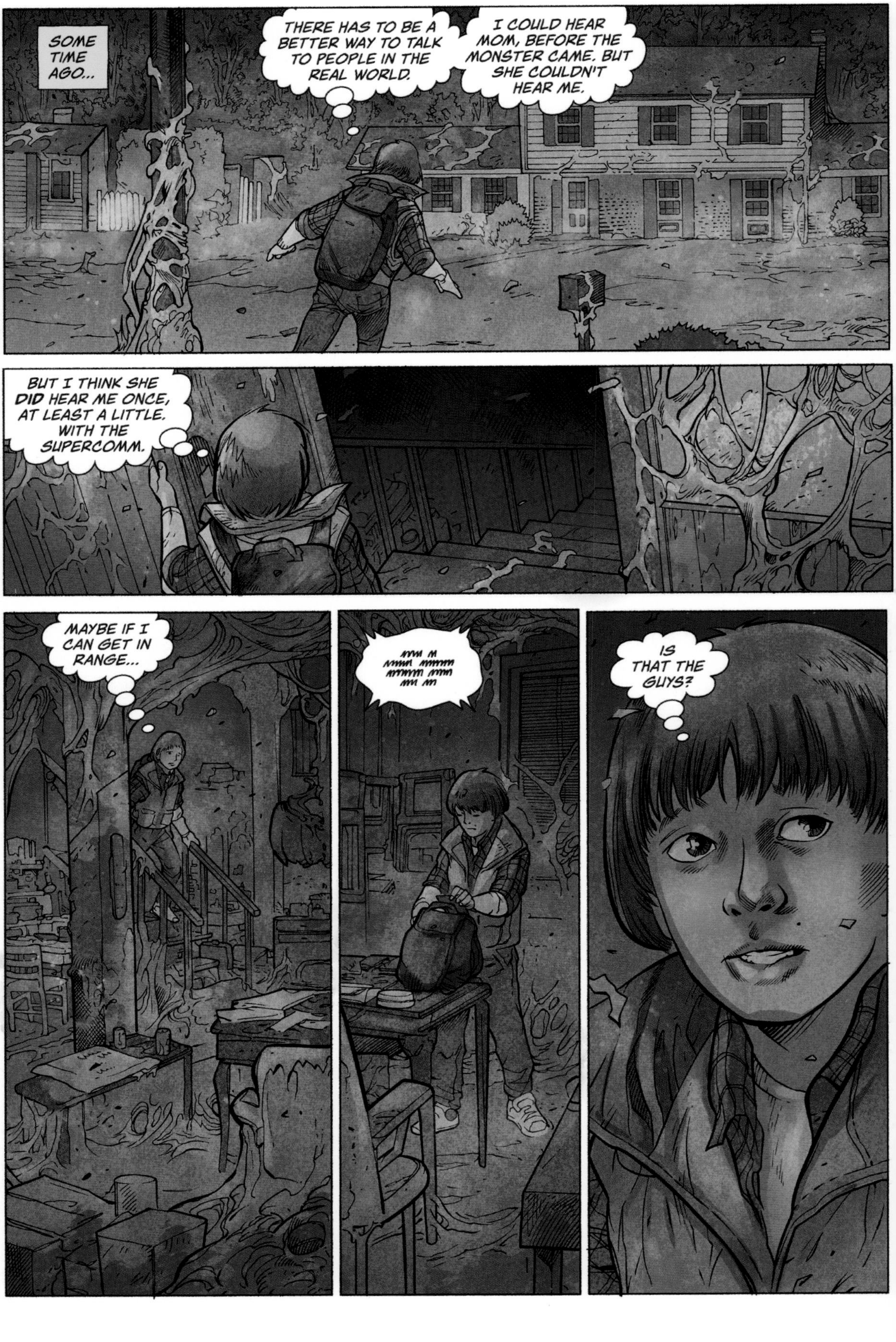
SOME TIME AGO...
THERE HAS TO BE A BETTER WAY TO TALK TO PEOPLE IN THE REAL WORLD.
I COULD HEAR MOM, BEFORE THE MONSTER CAME. BUT SHE COULDN'T HEAR ME.
BUT I THINK SHE DID HEAR ME ONCE, AT LEAST A LITTLE. WITH THE SUPERCOMM.
MAYBE IF I CAN GET IN RANGE...
IS THAT THE GUYS?

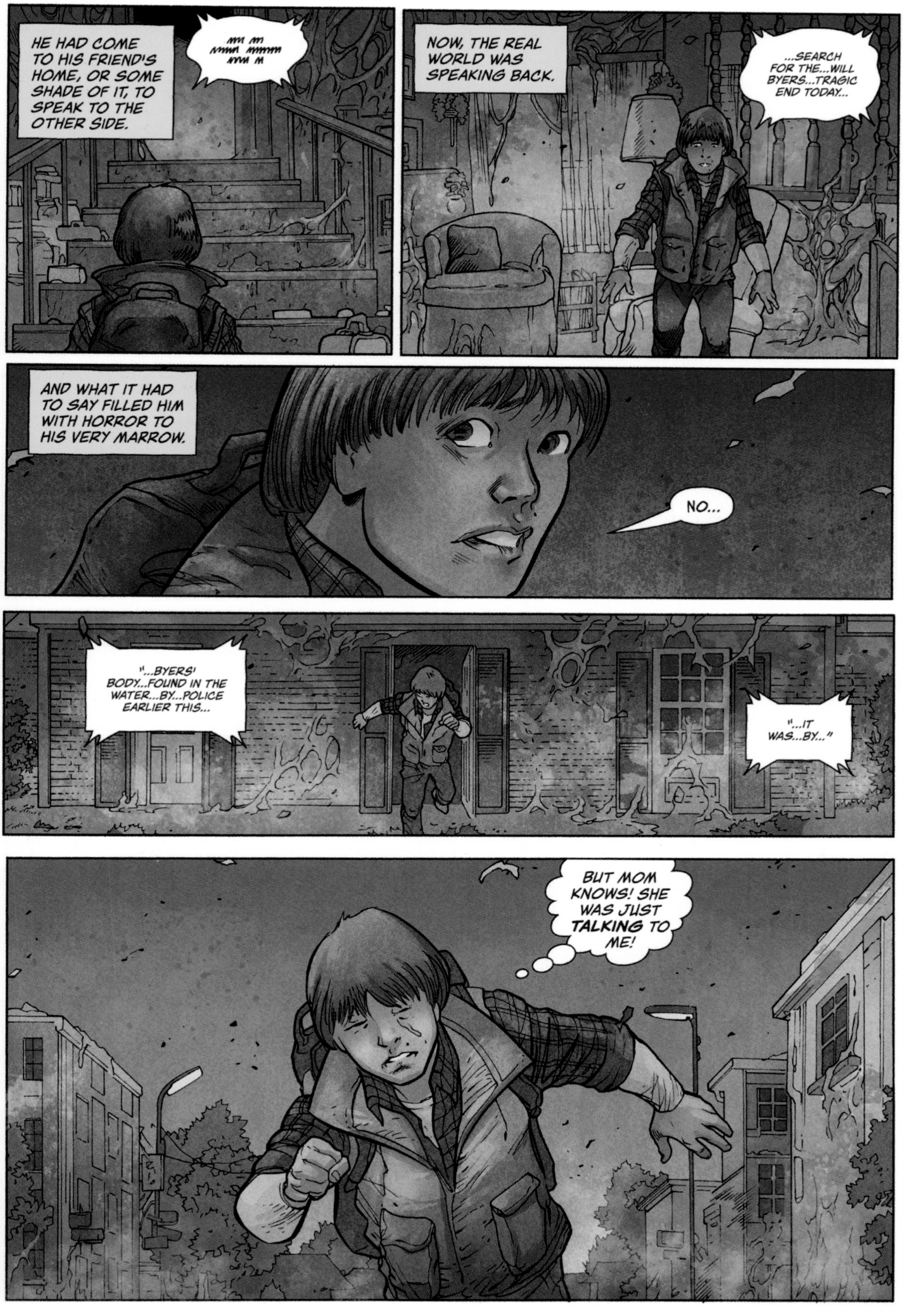
HE HAD COME TO HIS FRIEND'S HOME, OR SOME SHADE OF IT, TO SPEAK TO THE OTHER SIDE.
NOW, THE REAL WORLD WAS SPEAKING BACK.
...SEARCH FOR THE...WILL BYERS...TRAGIC END TODAY...
AND WHAT IT HAD TO SAY FILLED HIM WITH HORROR TO HIS VERY MARROW.
NO...
"...BYERS' BODY...FOUND IN THE WATER...BY...POLICE EARLIER THIS...
"...IT WAS...BY..."
BUT MOM KNOWS! SHE WAS JUST TALKING TO ME!

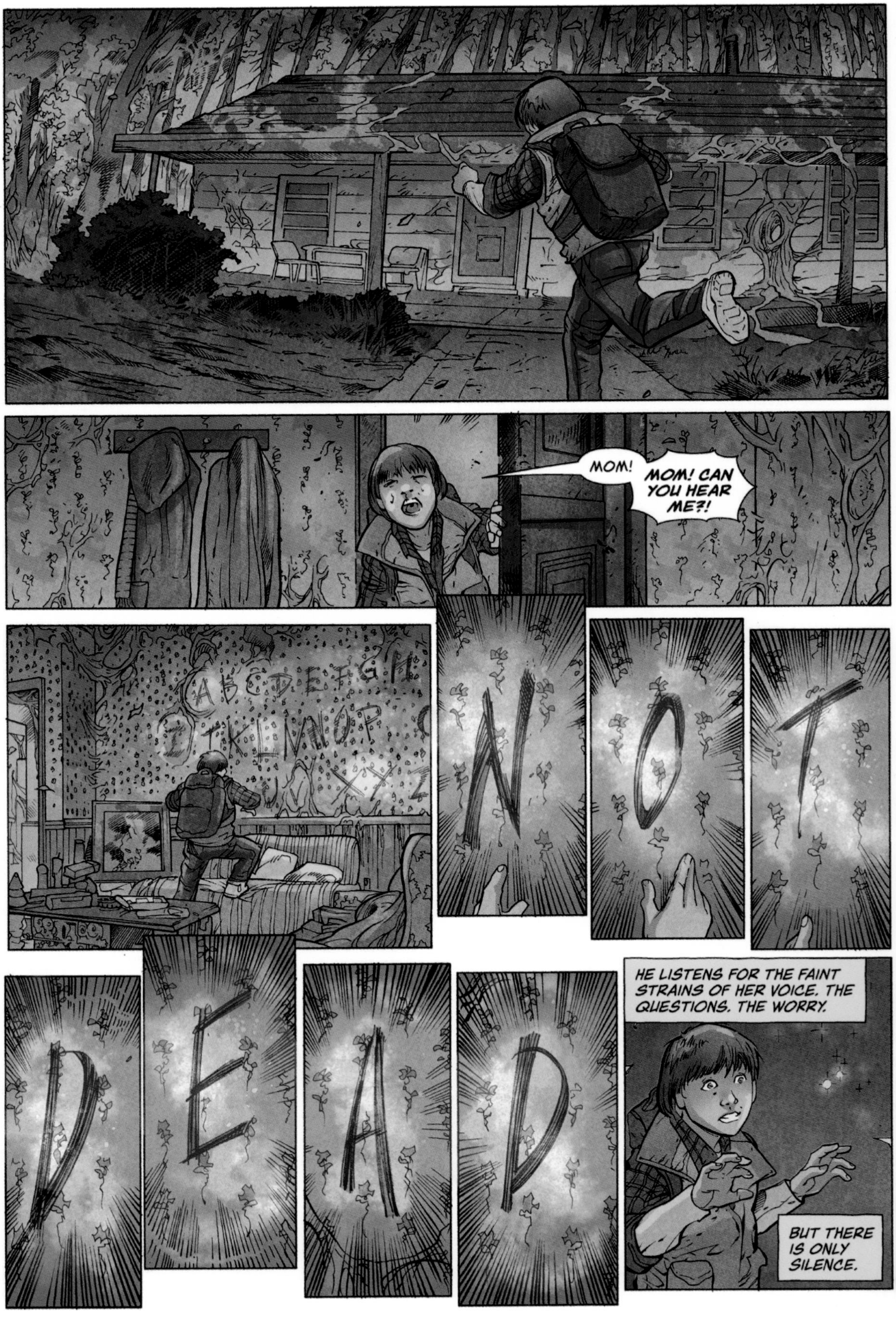
MOM!
MOM! CAN YOU HEAR ME?!
N
O
T
D
E
A
D
HE LISTENS FOR THE FAINT STRAINS OF HER VOICE. THE QUESTIONS. THE WORRY.
BUT THERE IS ONLY SILENCE.

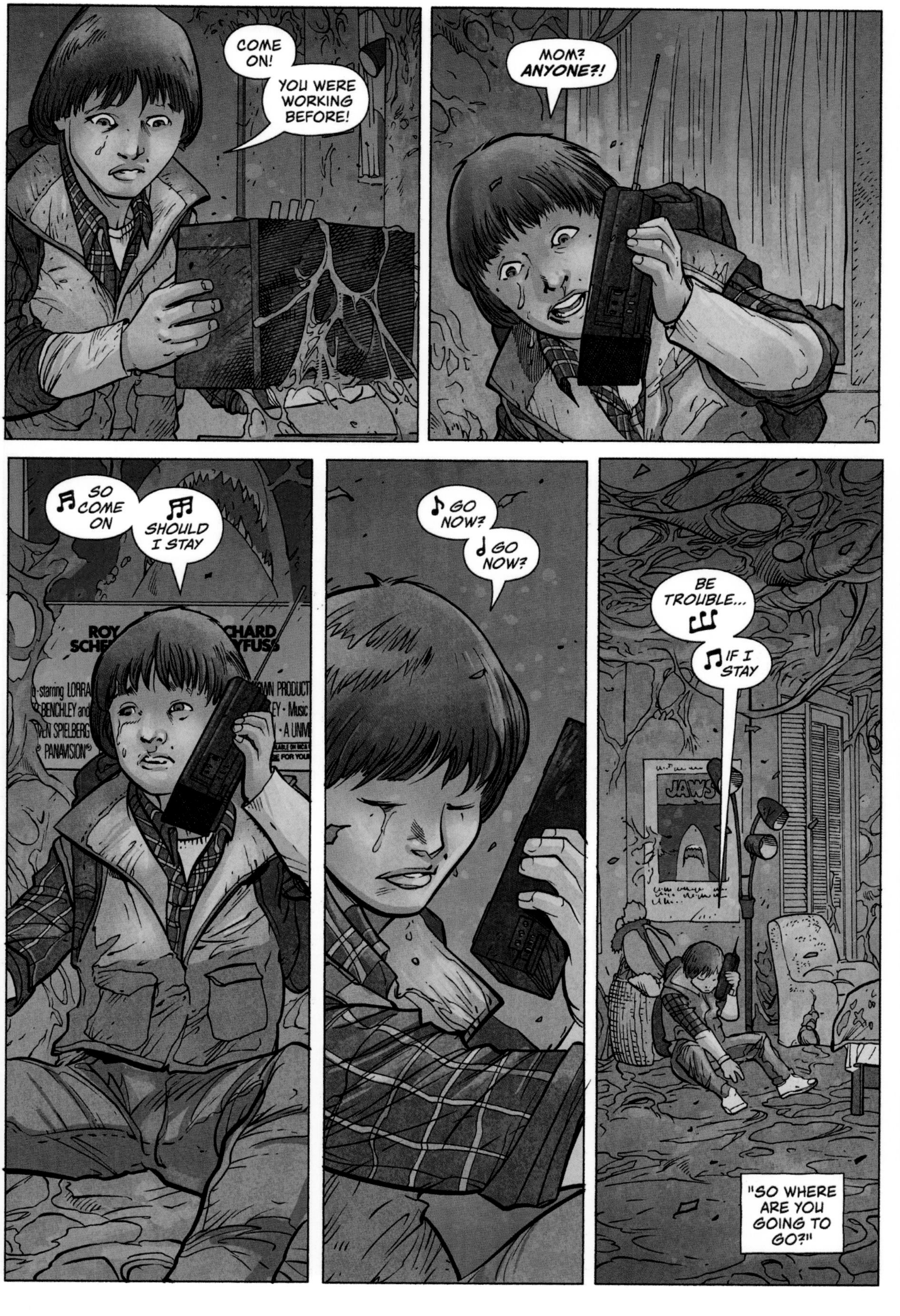
COME ON!
YOU WERE WORKING BEFORE!
MOM? ANYONE?!
SO COME ON
SHOULD I STAY
GO NOW?
GO NOW?
BE TROUBLE...
IF I STAY
JAWS
"SO WHERE ARE YOU GOING TO GO?!"

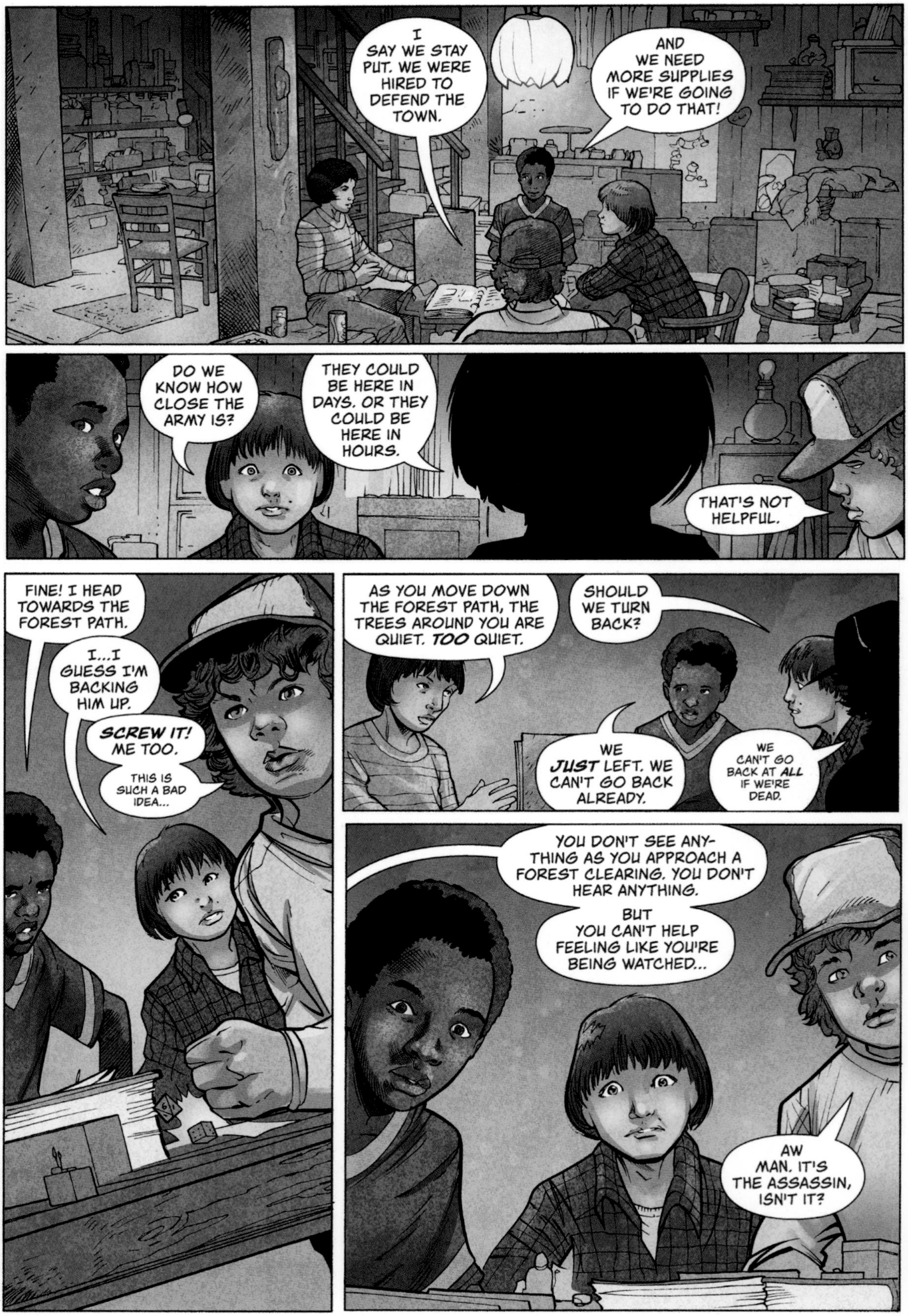
I SAY WE STAY PUT. WE WERE HIRED TO DEFEND THE TOWN.
AND WE NEED MORE SUPPLIES IF WE'RE GOING TO DO THAT!
DO WE KNOW HOW CLOSE THE ARMY IS?
THEY COULD BE HERE IN DAYS. OR THEY COULD BE HERE IN HOURS.
THAT'S NOT HELPFUL.
FINE! I HEAD TOWARDS THE FOREST PATH.
I...I GUESS I'M BACKING HIM UP.
SCREW IT! ME TOO.
THIS IS SUCH A BAD IDEA...
AS YOU MOVE DOWN THE FOREST PATH, THE TREES AROUND YOU ARE QUIET. TOO QUIET.
SHOULD WE TURN BACK?
WE JUST LEFT. WE CAN'T GO BACK ALREADY.
WE CAN'T GO BACK AT ALL IF WE'RE DEAD.
YOU DON'T SEE ANY-THING AS YOU APPROACH A FOREST CLEARING. YOU DON'T HEAR ANYTHING.
BUT YOU CAN'T HELP FEELING LIKE YOU'RE BEING WATCHED...
AW MAN. IT'S THE ASSASSIN, ISN'T IT?

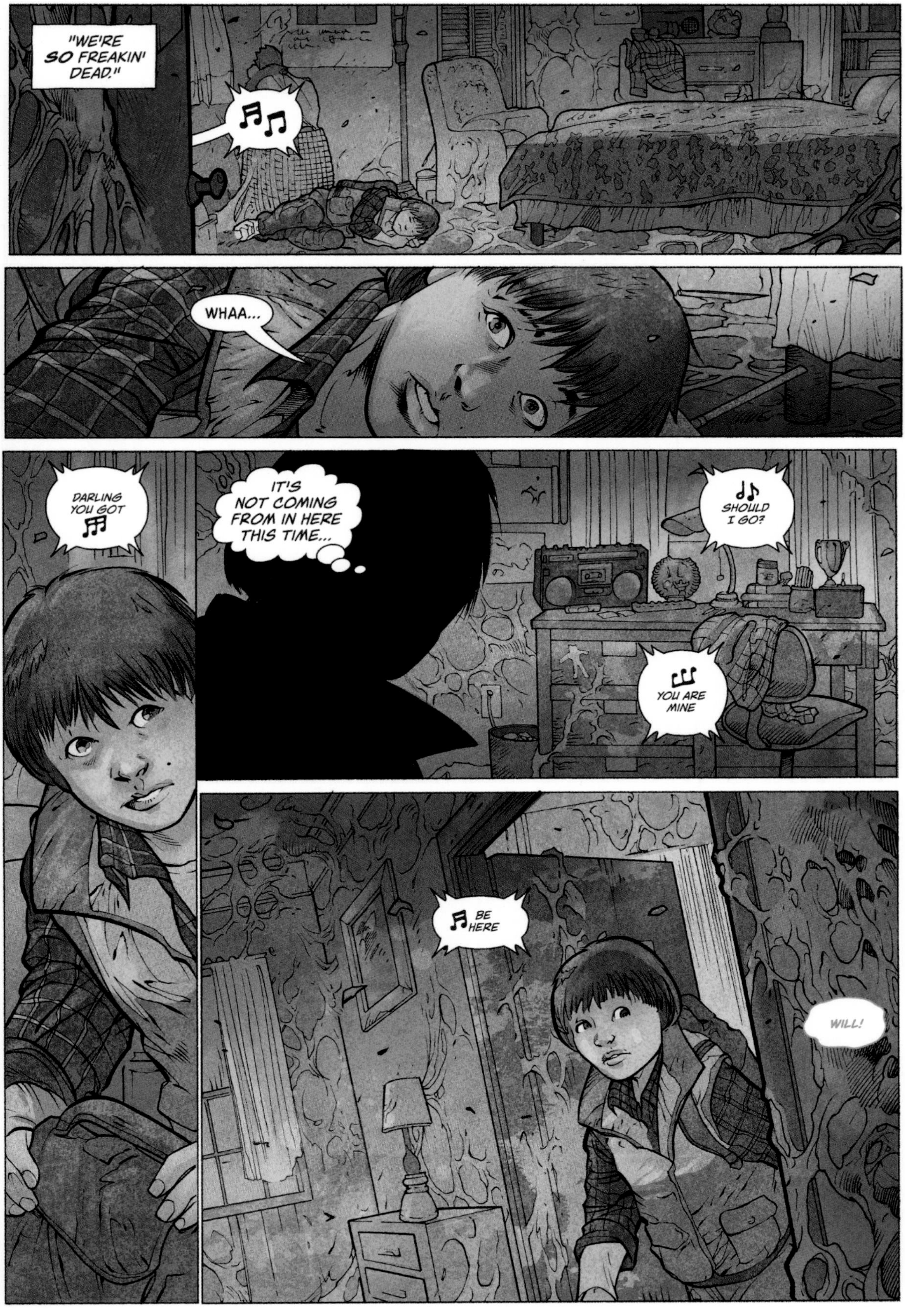
"WE'RE SO FREAKIN' DEAD."
♫♫
WHAA...
DARLING YOU GOT ♬
IT'S NOT COMING FROM IN HERE THIS TIME...
♩♪ SHOULD I GO?
YOU ARE MINE
♫ BE HERE
WILL!

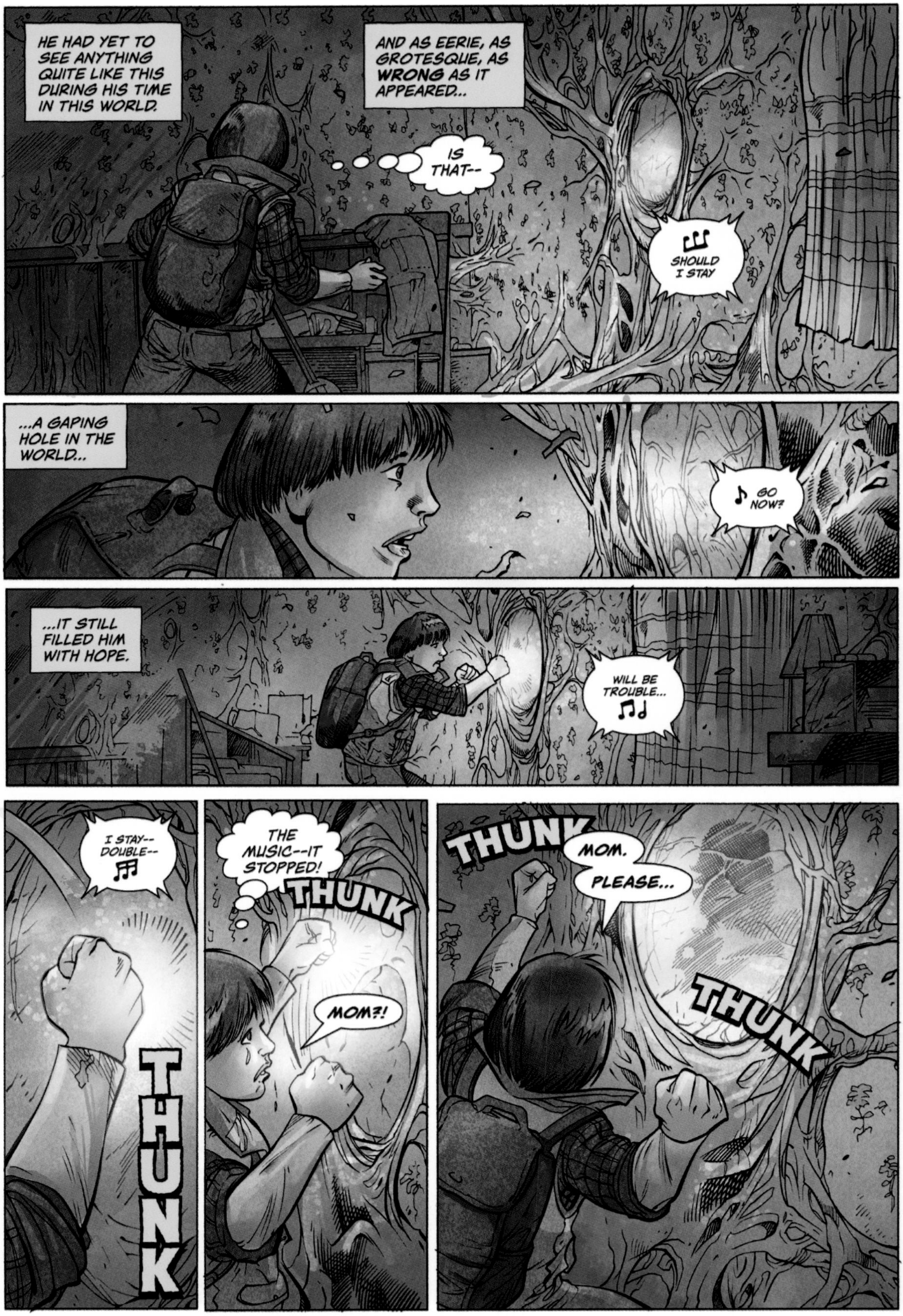
HE HAD YET TO SEE ANYTHING QUITE LIKE THIS DURING HIS TIME IN THIS WORLD.
AND AS EERIE, AS GROTESQUE, AS WRONG AS IT APPEARED...
IS THAT--
SHOULD I STAY
...A GAPING HOLE IN THE WORLD...
GO NOW?
...IT STILL FILLED HIM WITH HOPE.
WILL BE TROUBLE...
I STAY-- DOUBLE--
THUNK
THE MUSIC--IT STOPPED!
THUNK
MOM?!
THUNK
MOM.
PLEASE...
THUNK

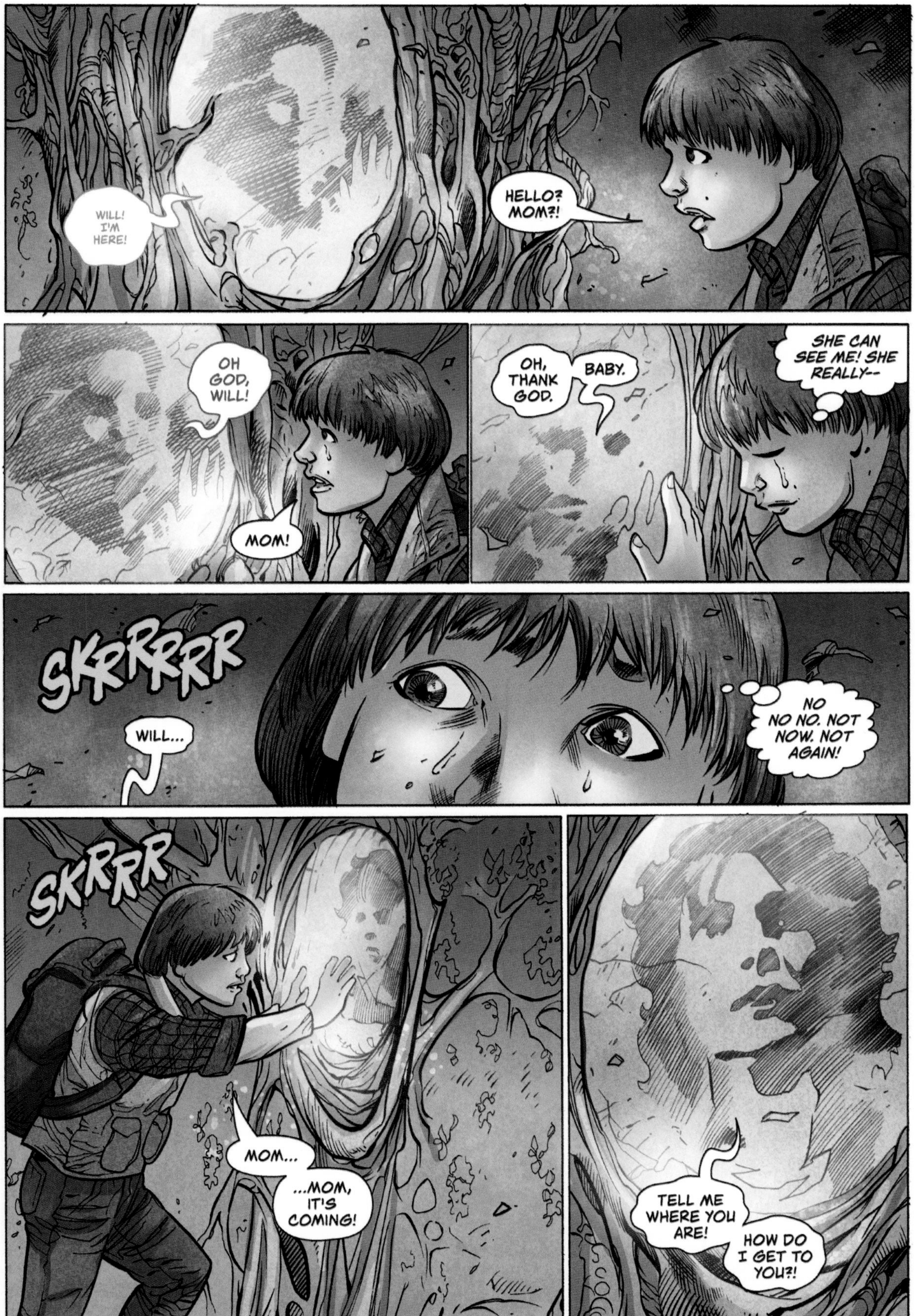
WILL! I'M HERE!
HELLO? MOM?!
OH GOD, WILL!
MOM!
OH, THANK GOD.
BABY.
SHE CAN SEE ME! SHE REALLY--
SKRRRRR
WILL...
NO NO NO. NOT NOW. NOT AGAIN!
SKRRR
MOM...
...MOM, IT'S COMING!
TELL ME WHERE YOU ARE!
HOW DO I GET TO YOU?!

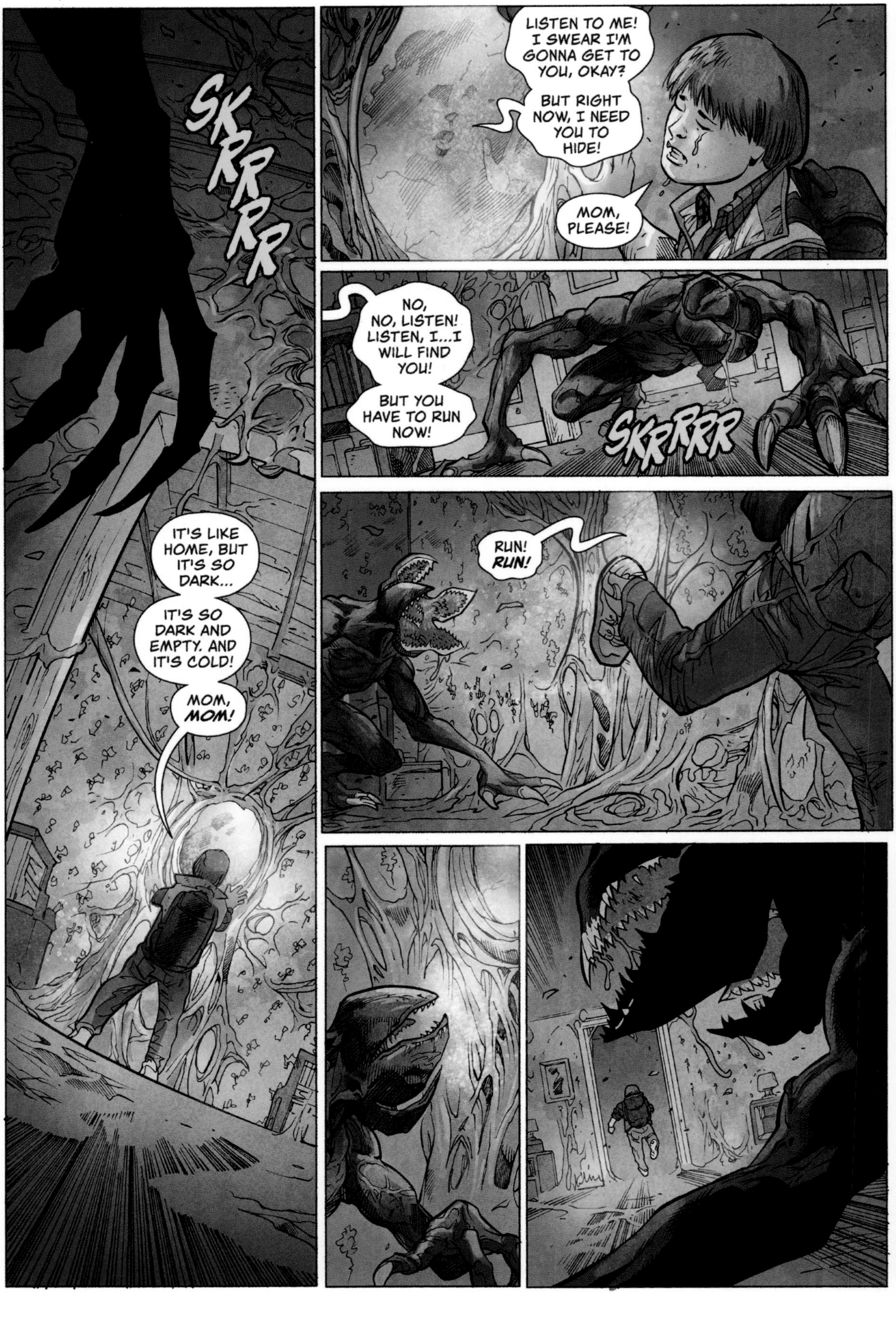
SKRRRR
IT'S LIKE HOME, BUT IT'S SO DARK...
IT'S SO DARK AND EMPTY. AND IT'S COLD!
MOM, MOM!
LISTEN TO ME! I SWEAR I'M GONNA GET TO YOU, OKAY?
BUT RIGHT NOW, I NEED YOU TO HIDE!
MOM, PLEASE!
NO, NO, LISTEN! LISTEN, I...I WILL FIND YOU!
BUT YOU HAVE TO RUN NOW!
SKRRRR
RUN! RUN!

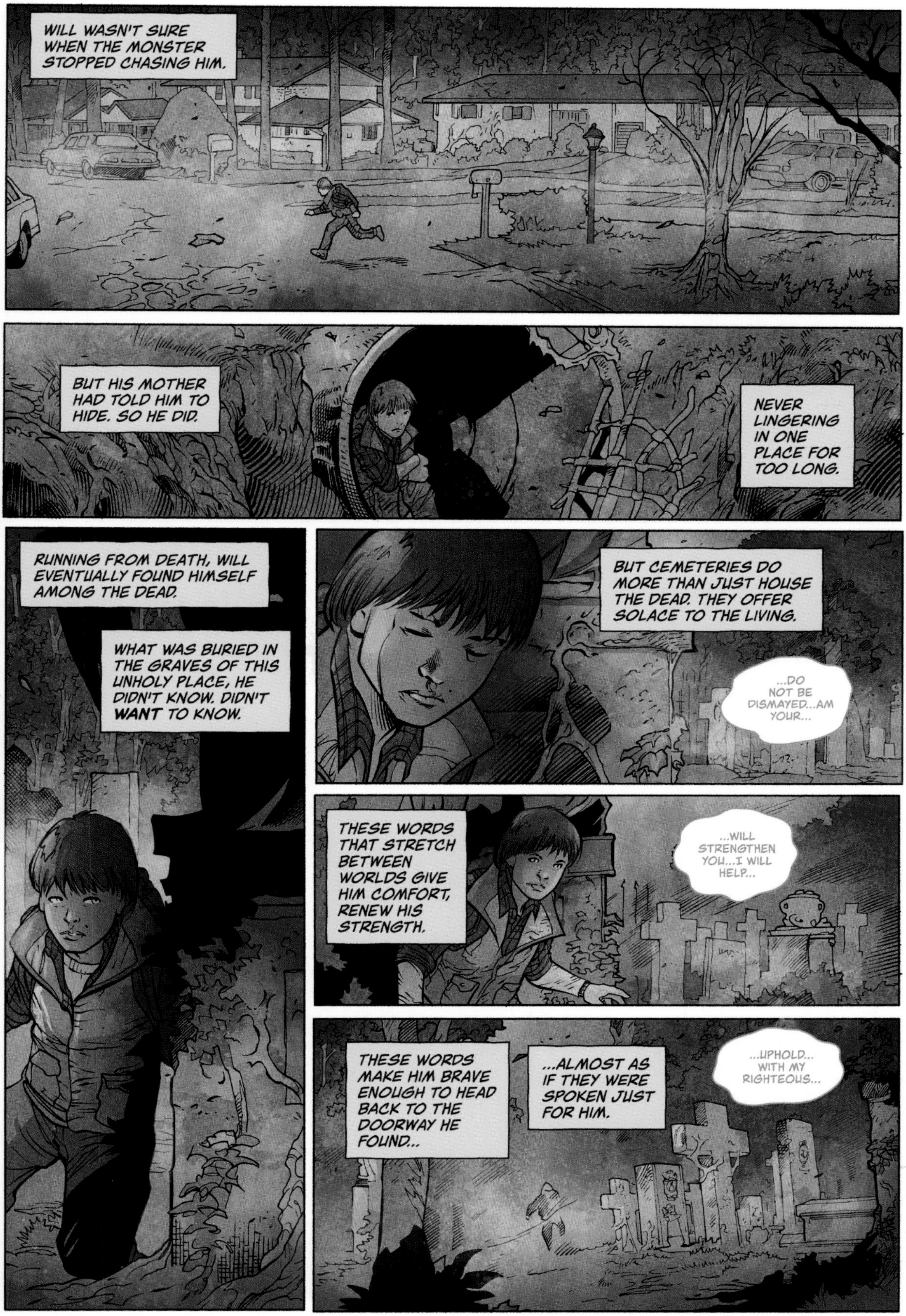
WILL WASN'T SURE WHEN THE MONSTER STOPPED CHASING HIM.
BUT HIS MOTHER HAD TOLD HIM TO HIDE. SO HE DID.
NEVER LINGERING IN ONE PLACE FOR TOO LONG.
RUNNING FROM DEATH, WILL EVENTUALLY FOUND HIMSELF AMONG THE DEAD.
WHAT WAS BURIED IN THE GRAVES OF THIS UNHOLY PLACE, HE DIDN'T KNOW. DIDN'T WANT TO KNOW.
BUT CEMETERIES DO MORE THAN JUST HOUSE THE DEAD. THEY OFFER SOLACE TO THE LIVING.
...DO NOT BE DISMAYED...AM YOUR...
THESE WORDS THAT STRETCH BETWEEN WORLDS GIVE HIM COMFORT, RENEW HIS STRENGTH.
...WILL STRENGTHEN YOU...I WILL HELP...
THESE WORDS MAKE HIM BRAVE ENOUGH TO HEAD BACK TO THE DOORWAY HE FOUND...
...ALMOST AS IF THEY WERE SPOKEN JUST FOR HIM.
...UPHOLD... WITH MY RIGHTEOUS...

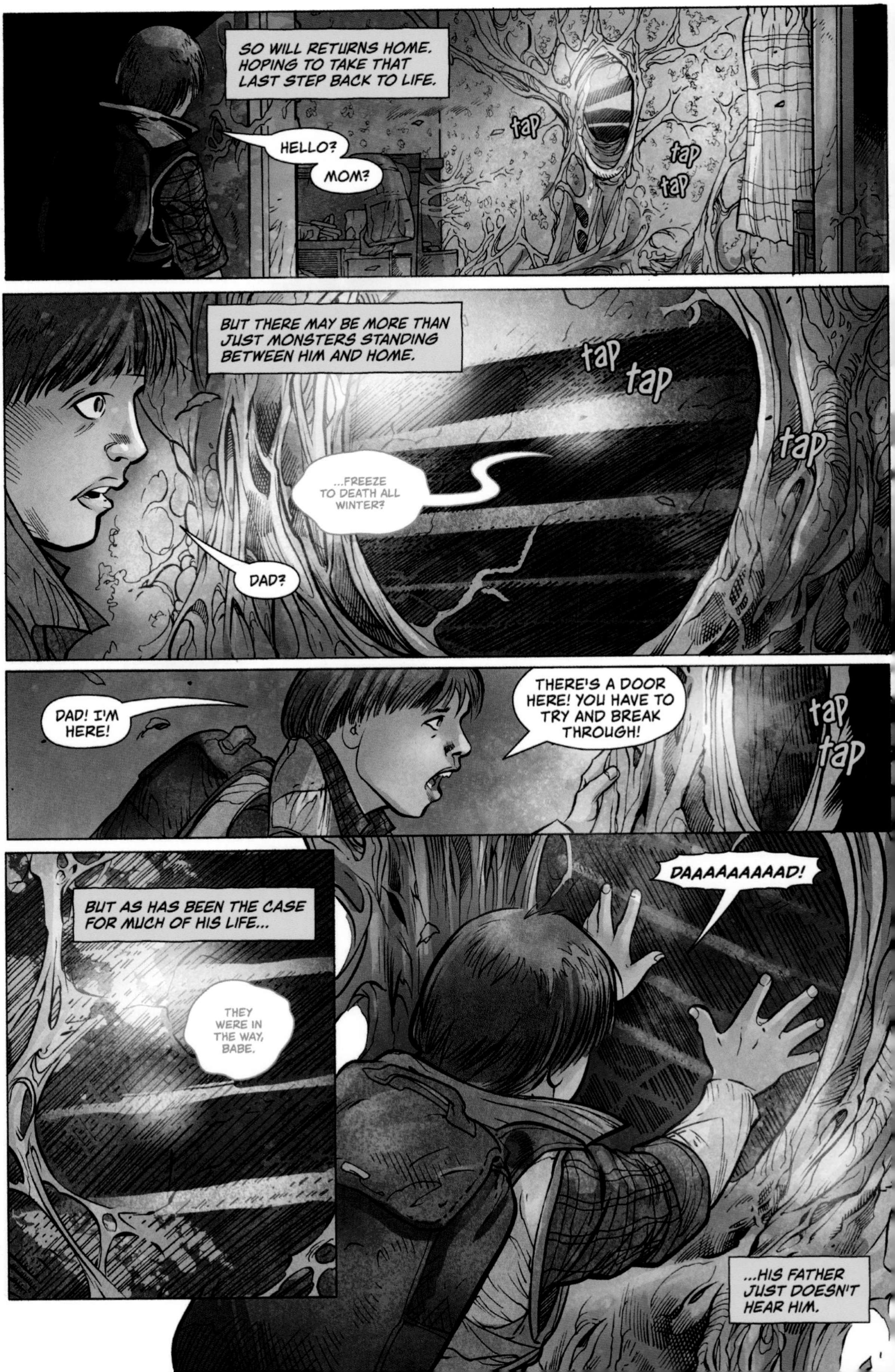
SO WILL RETURNS HOME. HOPING TO TAKE THAT LAST STEP BACK TO LIFE.
HELLO?
MOM?
tap
tap
tap
BUT THERE MAY BE MORE THAN JUST MONSTERS STANDING BETWEEN HIM AND HOME.
tap
tap
tap
...FREEZE TO DEATH ALL WINTER?
DAD?
DAD! I'M HERE!
THERE'S A DOOR HERE! YOU HAVE TO TRY AND BREAK THROUGH!
tap
tap
BUT AS HAS BEEN THE CASE FOR MUCH OF HIS LIFE...
DAAAAAAAAAD!
THEY WERE IN THE WAY, BABE.
...HIS FATHER JUST DOESN'T HEAR HIM.

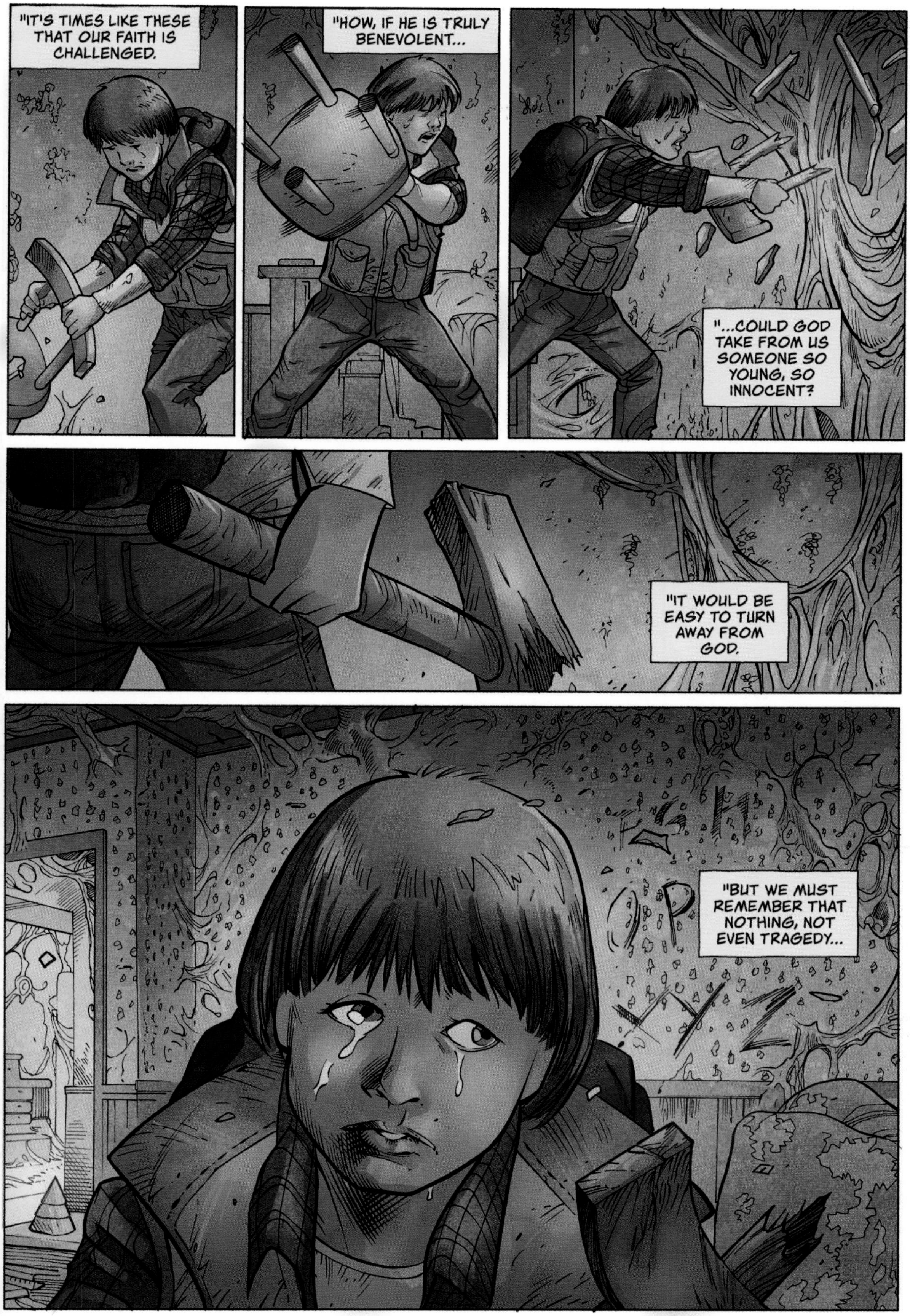
"IT'S TIMES LIKE THESE THAT OUR FAITH IS CHALLENGED.
"HOW, IF HE IS TRULY BENEVOLENT...
"...COULD GOD TAKE FROM US SOMEONE SO YOUNG, SO INNOCENT?
"IT WOULD BE EASY TO TURN AWAY FROM GOD.
"BUT WE MUST REMEMBER THAT NOTHING, NOT EVEN TRAGEDY...

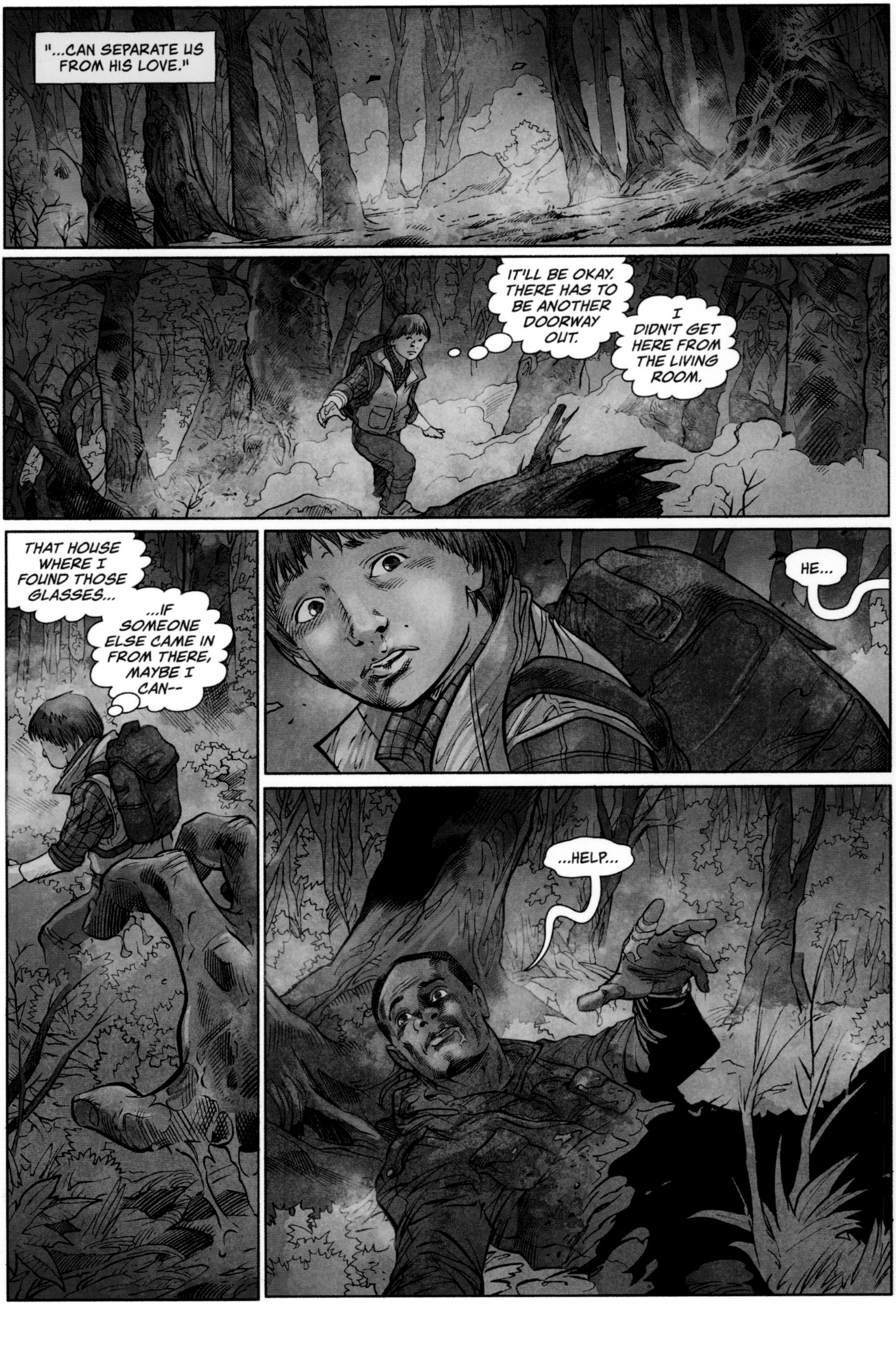
"...CAN SEPARATE US FROM HIS LOVE."
IT'LL BE OKAY. THERE HAS TO BE ANOTHER DOORWAY OUT.
I DIDN'T GET HERE FROM THE LIVING ROOM.
THAT HOUSE WHERE I FOUND THOSE GLASSES...
...IF SOMEONE ELSE CAME IN FROM THERE, MAYBE I CAN--
HE...
...HELP...

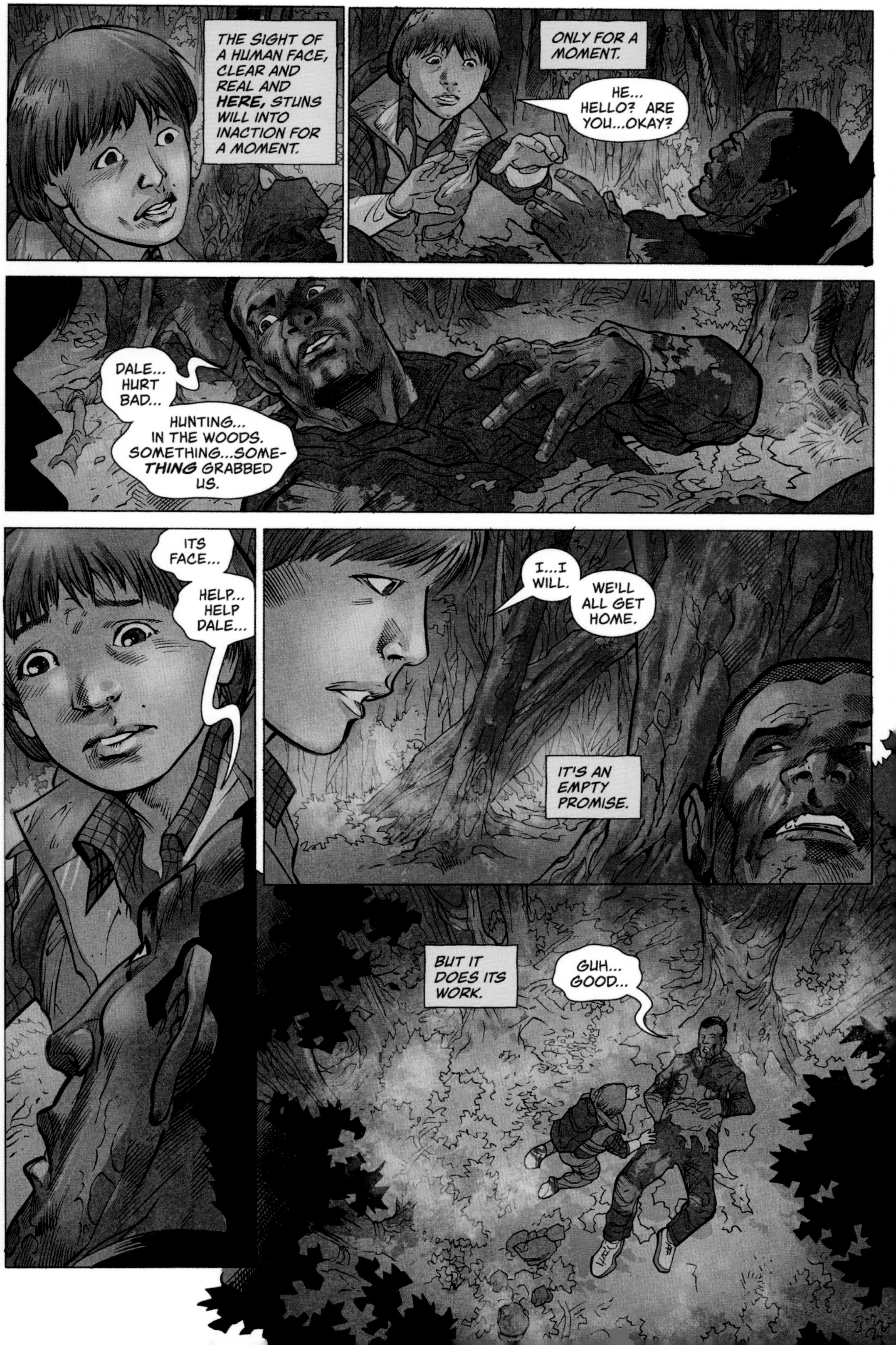
THE SIGHT OF A HUMAN FACE, CLEAR AND REAL AND HERE, STUNS WILL INTO INACTION FOR A MOMENT.
ONLY FOR A MOMENT.
HE... HELLO? ARE YOU...OKAY?
DALE... HURT BAD...
HUNTING... IN THE WOODS. SOMETHING...SOMETHING GRABBED US.
ITS FACE...
HELP... HELP DALE...
I...I WILL.
WE'LL ALL GET HOME.
IT'S AN EMPTY PROMISE.
BUT IT DOES ITS WORK.
GUH... GOOD...

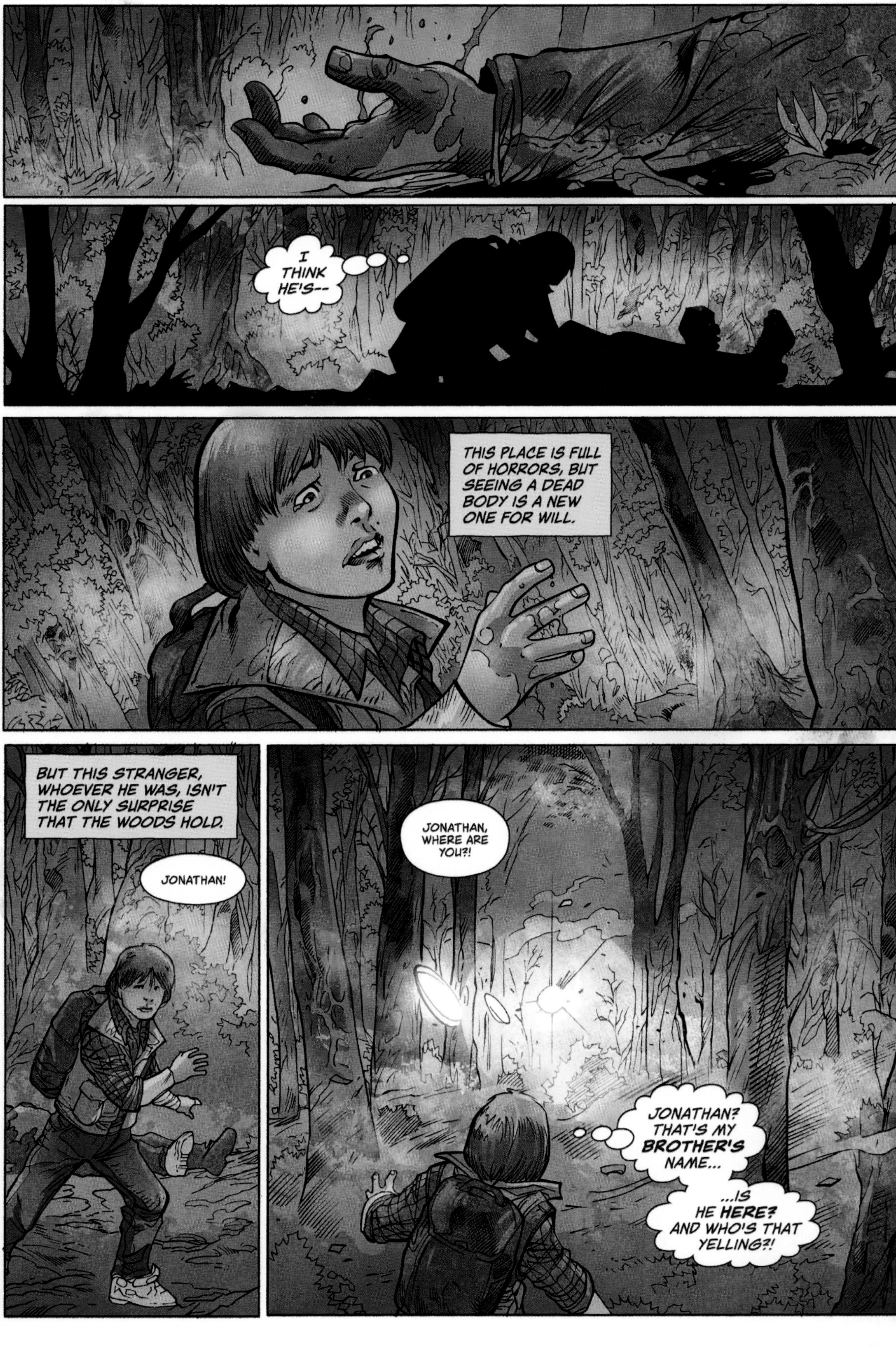

I THINK HE'S--
THIS PLACE IS FULL OF HORRORS, BUT SEEING A DEAD BODY IS A NEW ONE FOR WILL.
BUT THIS STRANGER, WHOEVER HE WAS, ISN'T THE ONLY SURPRISE THAT THE WOODS HOLD.
JONATHAN!
JONATHAN, WHERE ARE YOU?!
JONATHAN? THAT'S MY BROTHER'S NAME...
...IS HE HERE? AND WHO'S THAT YELLING?!

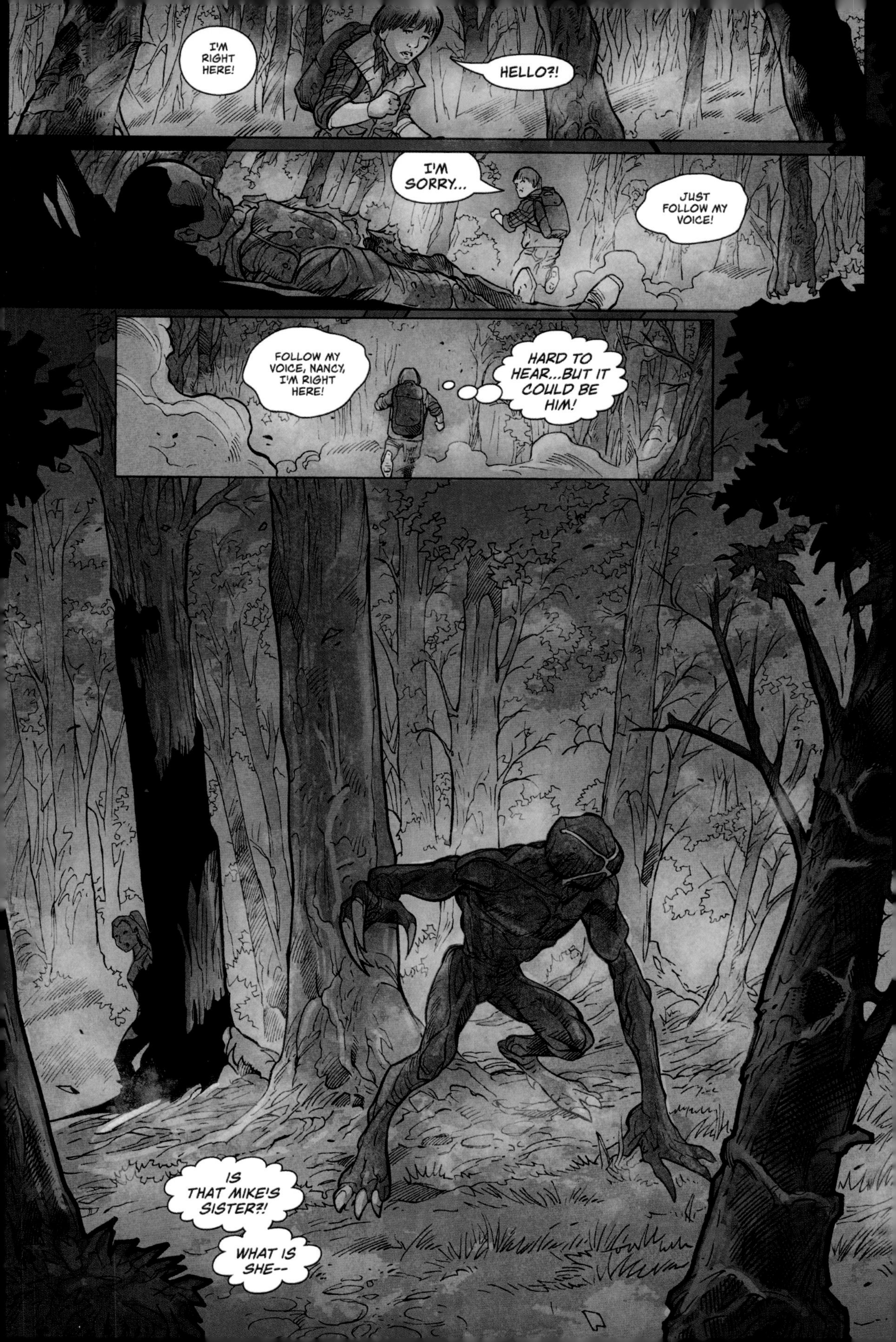
I'M RIGHT HERE!
HELLO?!
I'M SORRY...
JUST FOLLOW MY VOICE!
FOLLOW MY VOICE, NANCY, I'M RIGHT HERE!
HARD TO HEAR...BUT IT COULD BE HIM!
IS THAT MIKE'S SISTER?!
WHAT IS SHE--

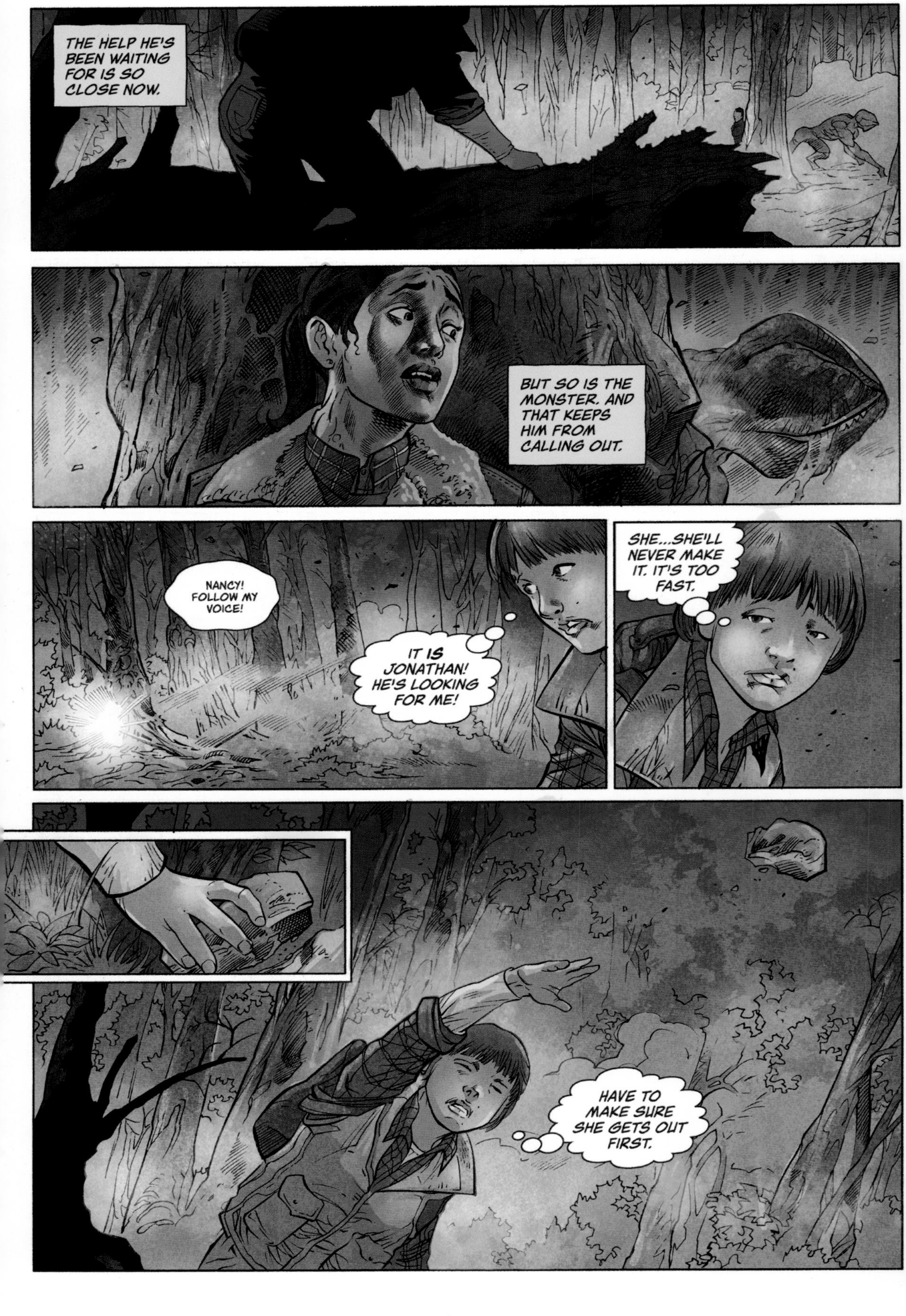
THE HELP HE'S BEEN WAITING FOR IS SO CLOSE NOW.
BUT SO IS THE MONSTER. AND THAT KEEPS HIM FROM CALLING OUT.
NANCY! FOLLOW MY VOICE!
IT IS JONATHAN! HE'S LOOKING FOR ME!
SHE...SHE'LL NEVER MAKE IT. IT'S TOO FAST.
HAVE TO MAKE SURE SHE GETS OUT FIRST.

TWAK

SKRAAAA!

GOTTA DRAW IT AWAY!

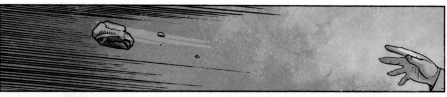

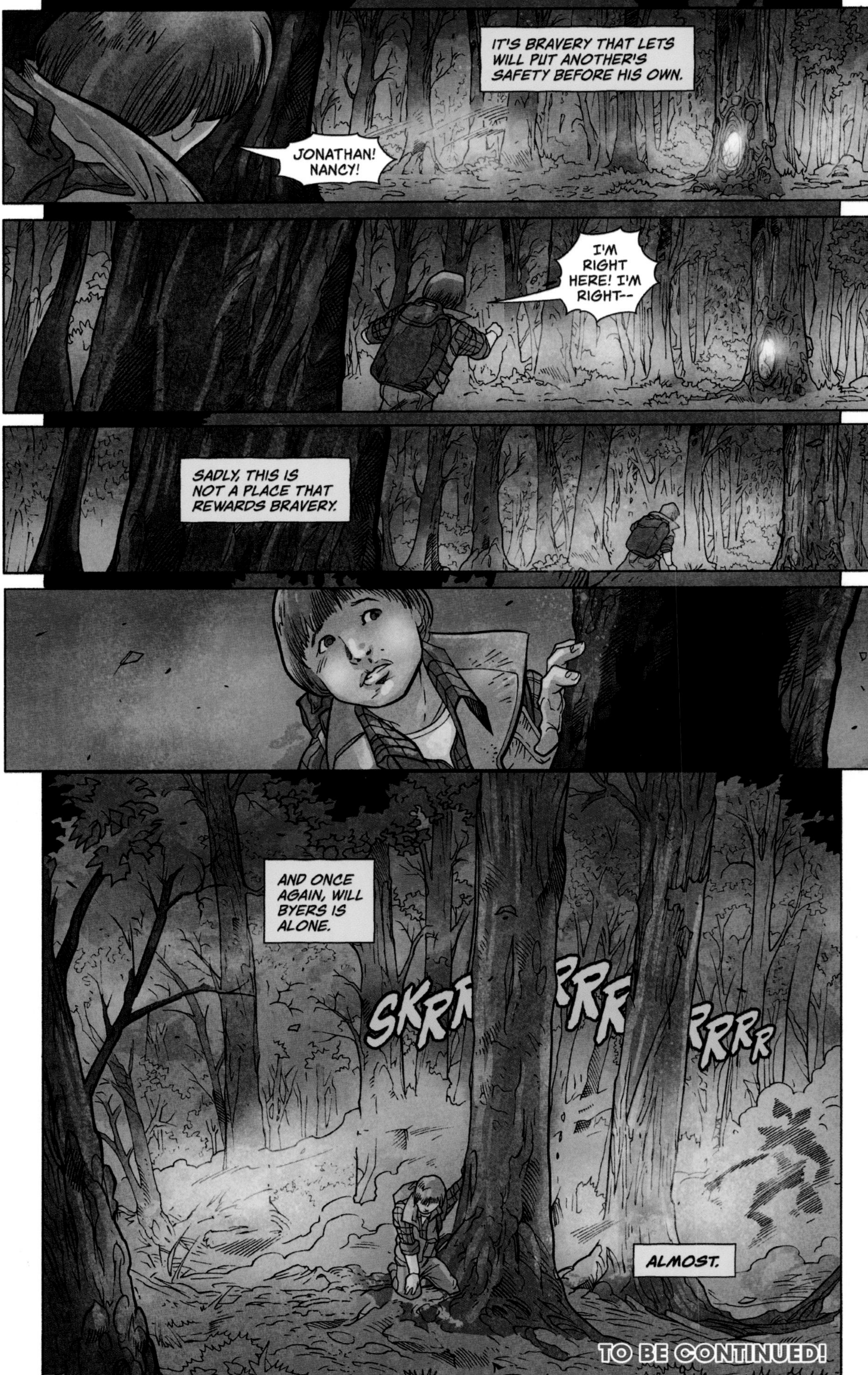
IT'S BRAVERY THAT LETS WILL PUT ANOTHER'S SAFETY BEFORE HIS OWN.
JONATHAN! NANCY!
I'M RIGHT HERE! I'M RIGHT--
SADLY, THIS IS NOT A PLACE THAT REWARDS BRAVERY.
AND ONCE AGAIN, WILL BYERS IS ALONE.
SKRRRRRRRRRR
ALMOST.
TO BE CONTINUED!